LITTLE RED RIDING HOOD

THE BREMEN TOWN MUSICIANS

Adapted by Jean-Pierre Enard

Illustrated by Gerda Muller

The Library of Dreams

LITTLE RED RIDING HOOD

Once upon a time there was a delightful little girl who was loved by everyone who saw her. The person who loved her most, however, was her Grandma. Her Grandma gave her anything she wanted.

One day she gave the little girl a red velvet hood. The hood suited her so well that she never wanted to take it off, even when she went to bed. From then on people always called her Little Red Riding Hood.

Translated by Pam Milward
Edited by Virginia Roundell

Published by Marshall Cavendish
Children's Books Limited,
58 Old Compton Street,
London WIV 5PA.

First published by Librairie Hachette
as *Le Petit Chaperon Rouge*
© Librairie Hachette, Paris 1979
English translation © Marshall Cavendish Ltd 1980

**Printed and bound by
Henri Proost, Turnhout, Belgium.**

ISBN 0 85685 844 7

One day her mother said to her, 'Little Red Riding Hood, here is some elderberry wine and a freshly baked cake. Take them to your Grandma because she is ill in bed. Go quickly now before the sun gets too hot. Be careful, and go straight there. Don't stray off the path. Don't stop to watch the birds. And most important of all, don't talk to strangers on the way. When you get there, don't forget to say "Good morning" to your Grandma.'

'I'll do exactly as you say,' replied Little Red Riding Hood. She put the cake and the wine in her basket and set off along the path.

Little Red Riding Hood's Grandma lived in the middle of a deep, dark forest.

Just as Little Red Riding Hood entered the forest she met a wolf.

She did not know that he was a wicked animal and so she was not afraid of him.

'Good morning, Little Red Riding Hood,' said the wolf.

'Good morning, wolf,' said Little Red Riding Hood, quite forgetting what her mother had said about not talking to strangers.

'Where are you going so early in the morning, Little Red Riding Hood?' said the wolf.

'To see my Grandma.'

'What have you got in your basket?'

'Elderberry wine and a cake. We baked the cake yesterday. I am taking it to my Grandma. She is ill and has to stay in bed.'

'Where does your Grandma live, Little Red Riding Hood?'

'About fifteen minutes walk from here, right in the middle of the forest. There are three big oak trees by her house. A little farther on there are some nut trees. It is quite easy to find if you follow the path.'

'What a charming little girl!' the wolf thought to himself. 'She should taste delicious. If I'm clever, I shall be able to eat Little Red Riding Hood and her Grandma too. I must make sure that I get to the house first.'

The wolf walked beside Little Red Riding Hood for a while. Then he said: 'Little Red Riding Hood! Look at those pretty flowers over there in the grass. You didn't even see them! Why don't you go and pick some for your Grandma? The birds are singing so happily today. Why don't you stop to listen to them? You are rushing along as if you were late for school. It's quite safe here in the forest.'

Little Red Riding Hood looked around. She saw the sunbeams dancing between the trees and brightly coloured flowers growing everywhere. 'Why shouldn't I stop to pick some flowers?' she thought. 'I'm sure Grandma would like some. It's still early, so there is plenty of time.'

Little Red Riding Hood left the path and started to look for flowers in the long grass. Each time she picked a flower she saw another even prettier one farther on . . . then another and another. She was so happy gathering flowers and listening to the birds that she forgot her mother's warning. She strayed deeper and deeper into the forest.

Meanwhile the wolf ran straight to Grandma's house.

He knocked on the door.

'Who is it?' said Grandma.

'Little Red Riding Hood,' said the wolf. 'I have brought you some elderberry wine and a cake. Please open the door.'

'Just lift the latch,' called Grandma. 'I'm too weak to get up.'

The wolf lifted the latch. The door swung open. The wolf leaped silently on to Grandma's bed and swallowed her up. Then he put on her clothes, perched her bonnet between his ears and pulled the sheets up to his chin. Then he drew the curtains round the bed and waited for Little Red Riding Hood to come.

Meanwhile Little Red Riding Hood had gathered so many flowers that she could carry no more. Suddenly, she remembered her Grandma. She picked up her basket and ran quickly back to the path.

When she arrived at her Grandma's house she was surprised to see that the door was open. She went inside and a strange feeling came over her. 'Oh dear!' she thought. 'Everything seems so odd today. I hope Grandma is all right.'

'Good morning!' she called. There was no reply. She went over towards the bed and drew back the curtains. There was her Grandma lying in bed with her bonnet drawn over her face. But Grandma did look strange today!

'Oh! Grandma, what big ears you have!' cried Little Red Riding Hood.

'All the better to hear you with,' replied the wolf.

'Oh! Grandma, what big eyes you have!'

'All the better to see you with, my dear.'

'Grandma! what big hands you have!'
'All the better to hold you with, my child.'
'But Grandma! your mouth is so big! And you have got such horrid, sharp teeth!'
'All the better to eat you with, Little Red Riding Hood!'

Hardly had the wolf said this when he leapt out of bed and gobbled up Little Red Riding Hood.

When the wolf had eaten her, he felt full and went back to bed. He soon fell asleep and began to snore.

Just then, a hunter passed the house. 'The old lady is snoring rather loudly today,' he thought to himself. 'Perhaps I had better go and see if she is all right.'

He went into the bedroom and discovered the wolf asleep in bed.

'You scoundrel! Fancy finding you here after I have hunted you for so long!' cried the hunter. He was just about to lift his rifle and kill the wolf when he remembered Grandma. What if the wolf had eaten her? She might still be alive. He put down his rifle and took some scissors out of his bag. He made two snips in the wolf's stomach. He caught sight of something red. The wolf did not wake so he made two more snips. Little Red Riding Hood jumped out. 'Oh! how frightened I was!' she said. 'It was so dark inside that horrible wolf!'

The hunter made another cut and they were able to pull Grandma out. She was still alive, but only just. The hunter asked Little Red Riding Hood to fetch some heavy stones. The three of them filled the wolf's stomach with the stones and the hunter sewed him up again. When the wolf woke he tried to leap out of bed. The stones made him so heavy that he crashed on the floor and was killed.

Then everyone was happy. The hunter took the wolf's skin and made himself a warm hat for the winter. Grandma ate the cake that Little Red Riding Hood had brought and felt much better. Little Red Riding Hood thought about all that had happened to her that day. She remembered her mother's warnings to her and decided never again to stray from the path.

Some months later Little Red Riding Hood took another cake to her Grandma. Again she met a wolf.

The wolf spoke to her as the first one had done. He too wanted to lure Little Red Riding Hood away from the path. But she did not make the same mistake again. She went straight to her Grandma's house and told her about the wolf. 'The wolf said "Good morning" to me most politely but he gave me such fierce looks! I'm sure that if I had not been on the path he would have gobbled me up at once.'

'Never mind,' said Grandma. 'We'll shut the door and put the bolt across so that the wolf can't come in.'

Soon there was a knock at the door and the wolf said: 'Open the door, Grandma. It is Little Red Riding Hood. I have brought you some cake.'

They did not reply or open the door. Then the grey beast silently padded round the house looking for a way to get in. At last he jumped on the roof. 'I'll wait here until it gets dark,' he thought. 'Little Red

Riding Hood will have to go home then. I'll follow her into the dark forest and eat her up.'

However, Grandma had guessed the wolf's plan. In front of the house was a large stone trough. 'Take the pail, Little Red Riding Hood,' said Grandma. 'Yesterday I cooked some sausages. I want you to take the water in which they cooked, and pour it into the trough.'

Little Red Riding Hood filled up the trough as her Grandma told her. Soon, the smell of boiled sausages reached the wolf. He sniffed the air, nostrils quivering, wondering where the smell came from. Alas! He leant out too far, lost his balance and slid down the roof. He fell into the trough below and was drowned.

Little Red Riding Hood went happily back home. No one ever tried to harm her again.

THE BREMEN TOWN MUSICIANS

Once upon a time there was a man who had a donkey. For years and years the donkey carried sacks of flour to the mill for his master. But now they were both growing old and the donkey could no longer carry a heavy load on his back. The man decided to get rid of the donkey to save himself the trouble of looking after it.

The donkey realized that his master no longer wanted him and ran away towards a nearby town called Bremen. There, he thought, he might learn to be a musician and play in the town band.

A short while later the donkey met a dog lying in the middle of the road. The dog was panting as if it was exhausted.

'Why are you panting so hard?' asked the donkey.

'Alas!' said the dog, 'I am old and every day I get weaker. I can't run fast enough to catch foxes any more. My master wanted to kill me so I ran away. What shall I do now?'

'I will tell you,' replied the donkey. 'I'm going to Bremen to become a musician and to play in the town band. If you come with me you could try to become a musician in the band too. I could play the lute and you could play the drums.'

The dog agreed and they went on together. They had not gone far when they met a cat. The cat was sitting on the road with a face as long as three days of rain.

'You don't look too happy, Puss,' said the donkey.

'Nor would you if your life was in danger!' replied the cat. 'I'm getting old and my teeth are no longer sharp. I would rather sit warming myself beside the fire than run around chasing mice. My mistress wanted to drown me but I escaped. Now I don't know what to do. What will happen to me?'

'Come with us to Bremen,' said the donkey. 'You know all about night music. You can play in the town band too.'

The cat thought this was a good idea and went along with the others.

Before long the three runaways passed a farmyard. A cock was sitting on the gate crowing at the top of its voice.

'You are deafening us with your cries,' said the donkey. 'What is the matter?'
'I am proclaiming a fine day,' said the cock. 'Today is the day on which the Blessed Mary washes the baby Jesus's nappies and hangs them out to dry. Tomorrow is Sunday and there will be guests at the house. The mistress is cruel and has told the cook to serve me up for dinner. Tonight they are going to cut off my head, so I am crowing with all my might while I still can.'

'You would do better to come with us, Red-Crest,' said the donkey. 'We are going to Bremen. At least you won't have your head cut off there. You have got a fine voice. When we play together we shall give a marvellous concert.' The cock was easily persuaded and all four went on their way together.

They could not reach Bremen in one day so they stopped for the night in a forest. The donkey and the dog lay down under a large tree. The cat and the cock settled down in the branches. The cock perched himself at the very top of the tree where he felt safest.

Before going to sleep he had a look round. He thought he spied a tiny light in the distance and called down to his companions. 'There must be a house over there where the light is.'

'If you are right,' said the donkey 'we ought to go there because this isn't a very comfortable place to spend the night.'

The dog agreed. He thought that he might find some meat in the house and perhaps a bone to chew. They all set off towards the light in search of food and a comfortable place to sleep. As they approached, the light grew larger and brighter and soon they came to a robbers' den.

The donkey, who was the tallest, put his head up to the window and looked inside.

'What can you see, Grey-Mane?' asked the cock.

'I can see food and drink on a table,' replied the donkey. 'There are robbers sitting round the table. They look very pleased with themselves.'

'We could just do with some of that food,' said the cock.

'Oh! If only we were inside!' said the donkey.

The animals wondered how they could drive away the robbers. At last they agreed on a plan. The donkey was to stand on his hind legs with his front hooves on the window-sill. The dog was to jump on the donkey's back, the cat was to climb up on the dog and the cock was to fly up to perch on the cat's head.

When they had arranged themselves, the donkey gave the sign and they began to perform. The donkey brayed, the dog barked, the cat mewed and the cock crowed. Then they broke the window panes and burst into the room. They made such a clatter that the robbers jumped out of their chairs. The robbers thought that a ghost had come in. They were so alarmed that they ran off into the forest in fright.

The four companions sat down to what was left of the meal. They ate as though they had not had a meal for a month.

When they had finished they put out the light. Each one looked for a suitable place to sleep. The donkey lay down by the dung-heap, the dog behind the door and the cat near the warm ashes in the hearth. The cock perched on a roof beam. They were all tired after their long walk and fell asleep immediately.

Some time after midnight the robbers looked back towards the house and saw that it was in darkness. All seemed quiet. 'We shouldn't have let ourselves be frightened away so easily,' said the chief. He called one of his men and sent him to investigate.

The man crept back to the house and found everything still. He went into the kitchen. He saw the cat's shining eyes and thought that they were glowing embers in the hearth. He struck a match to re-light the fire. But the cat did not give the robber

time to discover his mistake, and sank his claws into the man's face.

The robber was terrified and turned to run for the door. On the way he tripped over the dog. The dog jumped up and bit his leg. Once outside, the robber rushed across the yard. As he passed the dung-heap the donkey lashed out at him with his hind legs. All this noise woke the cock. 'Cock-a-doodle-doo! Cock-a-doodle-doo!' he crowed.

The robber ran back to his chief as fast as his legs would carry him. 'There's a horrible witch in the house who spat at me and scratched my face,' he said. 'By the door there's a man with a knife who cut my leg. In the yard there's a black monster. He beat me with a stick. Up on the roof there is a ghost who cried out "Bring me the robber!". I escaped as fast as I could.'

From that day on, the robbers never dared go near the house.

As for the four musicians, they were so happy in their new home that they never got to Bremen.

This ancient tale has been told many, many times, and at this moment someone, somewhere, is telling it over again.

PRINTED IN BELGIUM BY
proost
INTERNATIONAL BOOK PRODUCTION